to Olicorn!

FIRST PUBLISHED IN CANADA 2022 BY TUNDRA BOOKS

FIRST PUBLISHED IN GREAT BRITAIN 2022 BY FARSHORE

AN IMPRINT OF HARPERCOLLINSPUBLISHERS
I LONDON BRIDGE STREET, LONDON SEI 9GF

FARSHORE.CO.UK

HARPERCOLLINSPUBLISHERS
IST FLOOR, WATERMARQUE BUILDING, RINGSEND ROAD, DUBLIN 4, IRELAND

TEXT AND ILLUSTRATIONS COPYRIGHT © 2022 BEN CLANTON
THE AUTHOR AND ILLUSTRATOR HAVE ASSERTED THEIR MORAL RIGHTS

PUBLISHED BY ARRANGEMENT WITH TUNDRA BOOKS, AN IMPRINT OF PENGUIN RANDOM HOUSE
CANADA YOUNG READERS, A PENGUIN RANDOM HOUSE COMPANY

A CIP CATALOGUE RECORD OF THIS TITLE IS AVAILABLE FROM THE BRITISH LIBRARY

EDITED BY TARA WALKER AND PETER PHILLIPS
DESIGNED BY BEN CLANTON
THE ARTWORK IN THIS BOOK WAS RENDERED USING MAINLY PROCREATE AND ADOBE PHOTOSHOP.
THE TEXT WAS SET IN A TYPEFACE BASED ON HAND-LETTERING BY BEN CLANTON.

ISBN 978 0 7555 0018 5

PRINTED IN ITALY

I

CONTENTS

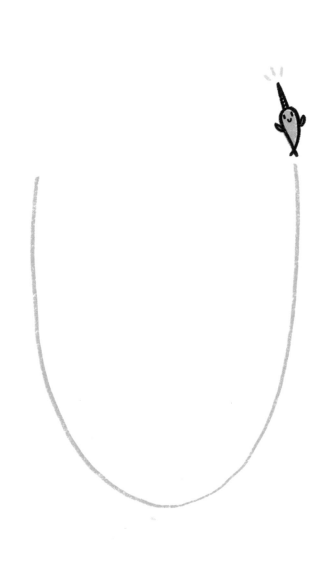

UNICORNS

NARWHALS
OF THE LAND

WELL, I'VE BEEN WONDERING . . .
WHAT EXACTLY IS A UNICORN?

HAVE YOU ACTUALLY EVER
SEEN ONE BEFORE?

Oooh!
Hmm!

I HAVEN'T.
BUT I GUESS
THEY'RE
PRETTY
MUCH
THE
NARWHALS
OF THE
LAND!

MEET ME BY THE BIG BEACH AT HIGH TIDE TONIGHT!

OH! BUT THAT'S WAY PAST MY BEDTIME!

IT'S ALWAYS A GOOD TIME FOR AN ADVENTURE, AND AN ADVENTURE IS ALWAYS A GOOD TIME!

UM, I'M NOT SO SURE ABOUT THAT... WAIT! WHAT ADVENTURE?

13

FUN FACTS
ABOUT REAL UNICORNS?

ELASMOTHERIUM (A.K.A. THE SIBERIAN UNICORN) IS AN EXTINCT TYPE OF RHINOCEROS THAT WAS SIMILAR IN SIZE TO A MAMMOTH AND HAD A HUGE HORN ON ITS FOREHEAD.

RHINO? I'M WOOLLY SOME SORT OF UNICORN!

NOT MUCH IS KNOWN ABOUT THE HORN-LIKE PROTRUSION OF UNICORNFISH.

WHAT I KNOW IS I LOOK AWESOME!

THE HUMMINGBIRD HAWK-MOTH HAS A "HORN" WHEN IT'S A LARVA!

BUT . . . IT ISN'T ON MY HEAD!

MORE UNIQUE UNICORNS?

TEXAS UNICORN MANTIS

LOOKS LIKE IT HAS ONE HORN BUT ACTUALLY HAS TWO.

JUST MEANS I'M TWICE AS AWESOME!

NARWHAL SHRIMP A.K.A. UNICORN SHRIMP

CALL ME SHRIMPICORN!

AND, OF COURSE, NARWHALS! NOT ALL HAVE A HORN-LIKE TUSK. BUT SOME HAVE TWO!

TWO COOL!

HAVE THIS WISH
I FISH TONIGHT

YAWN

WELL, WE'RE BY
THE BIG BEACH.
NOW WHAT, NARWHAL?

TIME TO SAY HI
TO A STELLAR
FRIEND!

SOMETIME SOON, FOR SHORE! BUT JUST NOW I HAVE ANOTHER WISH . . . I THINK IT WOULD BE GRAND TO WALK ON LAND.

I'D BE HAPPY TO GIVE YOU A LEG UP! YOU REMEMBER THE WORDS, RIGHT?

STAR LIGHT,
STAR BRIGHT,
FIRST STAR
I SEE TONIGHT.
I WISH I MAY,
I WISH I MIGHT,
HAVE THE WISH
I WISH
TONIGHT.

I WISH WE WERE WISHING FOR MORE SLEEP.

THAT WAS A GAS! WANT
TO ADD ANYTHING MORE?

THESE LEG THINGS SURE
ARE OUTSTANDING!
MORE? SURE! HOW ABOUT . . .

WHA?!
I CAN'T EVEN . . .
WHAT'S NEXT?! HAIR?!

wibble
wobble

GOOD IDEA, JELLY! HAIR!

WELL, THAT'S JUST . . . GRAND.

29

YIKES! WELL . . . IT LOOKS LIKE THOSE LEGS AREN'T SO STEADY. I'M NOT SURE YOU'RE READY. LET'S CALL IT A NIGHT?

I'M ALL RIGHT!

I JUST NEED TO PUT IN A LITTLE PRACTICE!

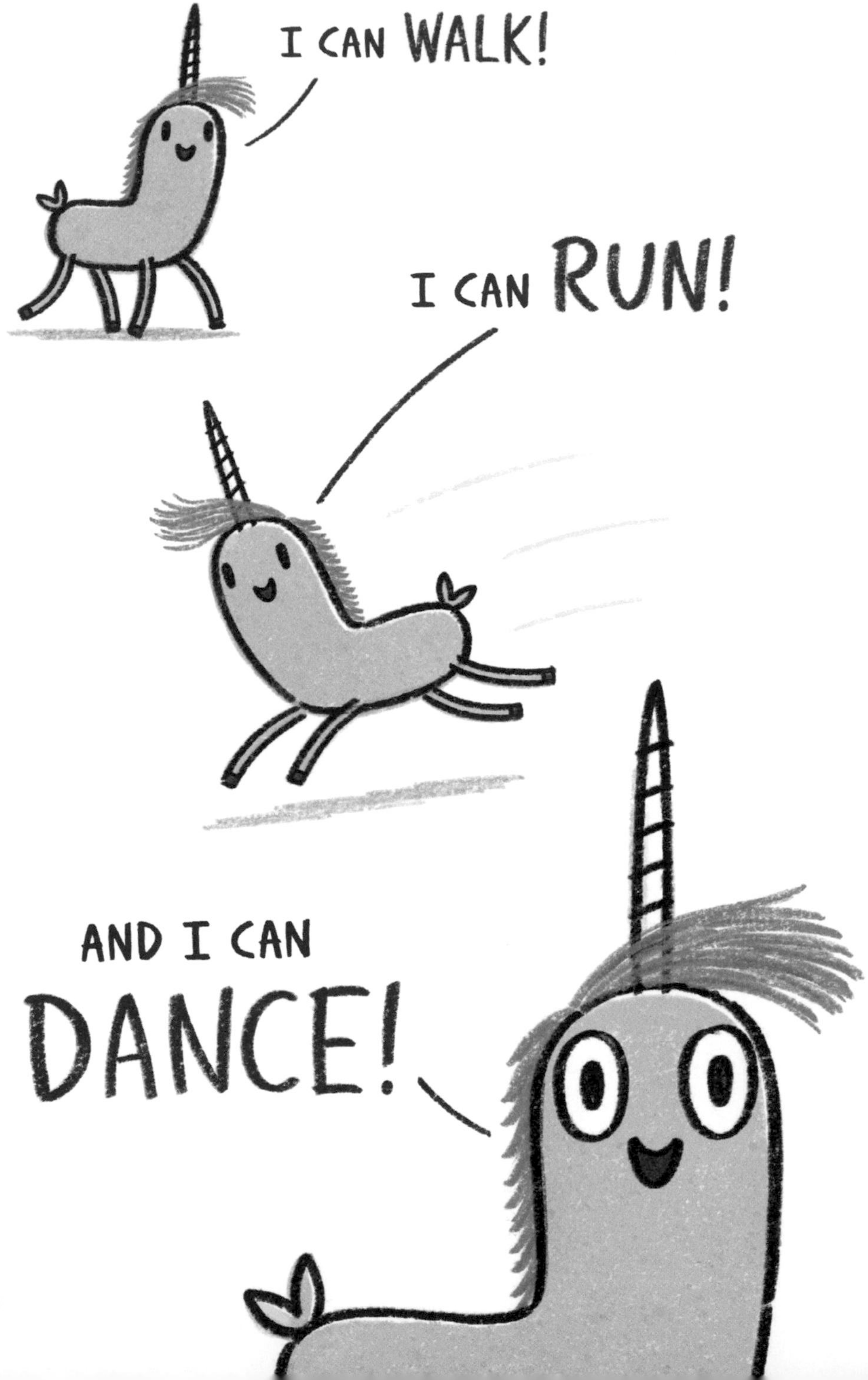
I CAN WALK!
I CAN RUN!
AND I CAN
DANCE!

THE NARWHALICORN DANCE

PRANCE!
PRANCE!

PRANCE!

I'M DOING
A DANCE!

ON THE
LAND!

ON THE
SAND!

ISN'T
IT GRAND?

YES!

PRANCE!
PRANCE!

PRANCE!

I'M
DOING
A...

DANCE!

NARWHALICORN
IS
OUT-OF-THIS-
WORLD!

IF YOU'RE SEEKING UNICORNS, THEY'RE PRETTY RARE AROUND HERE. YOU SHOULD TRY THE UNICORN PLANET!

UNICORN PLANET?

THIS IS OUT-OF-THIS-WORLD!

THIS IS OUT-OF-MY-COMFORT-ZONE!

THERE IT IS!

ISN'T IT UNBELIEVABLY
BEAUTIFUL?

EMPHASIS ON THE
UNBELIEVABLE.

NARWHALICORN!

HI! I'M PLATYCORN!

YETICORN!

CLOUDYCORN!!!

PANDICORN!

HORSICORN!

WELCOME TO THE
UNICORN PLANET!
WHERE EVERYONE IS
A UNICORN!

EVERYONE?

YEP! THAT'S RIGHT, JELLYCORN!

UH . . . BUT . . . NO HORN?

SOME HORNS ARE INVISIBLE. BUT THAT DOESN'T MEAN YOU AREN'T A UNICORN.

GET IT?

UM . . . NOT SO MUCH. NO.

LET THE PARTYCORN BEGIN!

PARTYCORN!

PARTYCORN!

I JUST WISH
I COULD GO HOME...

I'M BACK! PHEW!

WAIT! WAS THAT ALL JUST ONE WILD AND WEIRD DREAM?

NO . . . THAT WAS TOO BIZARRE FOR ME TO EVER DREAM UP.

NARWHALICORN SURE
SEEMED HAPPY UP THERE.

I WONDER IF THEY'LL
EVER COME HOME . . .

MEANWHILE, BACK ON THE UNICORN PLANET . . .

WOW. JELLYCORN IS A BIT OF A PARTY POOPER.

ACTUALLY, JELLY IS USUALLY A PARTY TROOPER! BUT . . .

I THINK I MIGHT NOT HAVE BEEN A SUPER LISTENER.

I WISH I COULD MAKE IT UP TO JELLY.

MAYBE I SHOULD HAVE WISHED FOR BIGGER EARS INSTEAD!

I, NARWHAL, HEREBY PLEDGE TO BE A BETTER LISTENER.

THANKS, CHUM. IT'S OKAY.

YOU PICK THE NEXT ADVENTURE?

SURE! BUT TOMORROW. THE FURTHEST I WANT TO ADVENTURE RIGHT NOW IS TO MY SEABED.

AHOY, JELLY!
WHAT ARE WE
UP TO TODAY?

GOOD MORNING,
NARWHAL! WANT
TO BUILD A
SANDCASTLE?

SURE THING!
THAT SOUNDS LIKE
AN OUTSANDING IDEA!

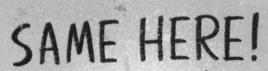

SAME HERE!

WHOA!
NARWHAL,
THAT'S ONE
WAFFLEY
SWEET
TOWER!

THANKS,
JELLY!

YOU SOMEHOW MAKE
EVEN THE ORDINARY
ADVENTURES
EXTRAORDINARY!

POOF! POOF!
POOF! POOF!
POOF! POOF!
POOF! POOF!

SPEAKING OF EXTRAORDINARY . . .

AHOY, STAR, PLATYCORN, YETICORN, CLOUDYCORN, PANDICORN, ROBOCORN AND HORSICORN!

THEY ALL WISHED TO COME AND SEE THE SEA!

HI . . .

WANT TO JOIN US ON ANOTHER ADVENTURE?

MAYBE SOME OTHER TIME! WE'RE IN THE MIDDLE OF MAKING CASTLES RIGHT NOW.

NARWHAL, IT'S OKAY . . .

THUNK

THIS JELLYCORN
SLEPT SOUNDLY
AND IS NOW READY FOR,
WELL, NOT ANYTHING,
BUT ... SOMETHING!
SO LONG AS WE CAN
STAY IN THE
WATER TODAY?

AS YOU WISH!
OR SHOULD I SAY,
AS YOU JELLYFISH!

PARTYCORN!
PARTYCORN!

EVERYBODY
PARTYCORN!